Rudolph the Red-Nosed Reindeer

Published by arrangement with
Modern Curriculum Press, Inc.

Adapted from the story
by Robert L. May

GOLDEN® and GOLDEN® & DESIGN
are trademarks of Western Publishing Company, Inc.

A GOLDEN® BOOK
Western Publishing Company, Inc.
Racine, Wisconsin 53404

Rudolph was unhappy because Santa's reindeer laughed at his shiny red nose.

The reindeer made fun of Rudolph and called him names.

Snowflake Designs

Santa's elves and reindeer loved to play in the snow. The snowflakes were big and fluffy, and each one was different. Make up your own dot-to-dot designs with these snowflakes.

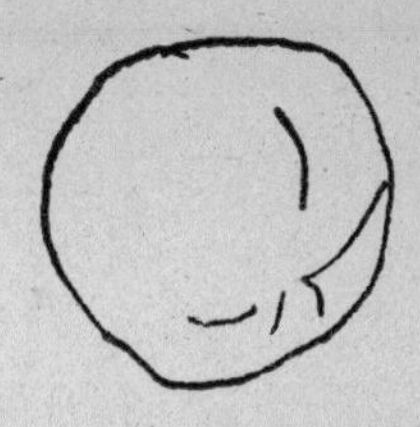

Snowball

How many words can you make using only the letters in SNOWBALL?

Some possible answers: no, so, an, as, on, ow, bow, now, all, sow, son, sob, ban, low, law, lab, nob, saw, nab, owl, was, won, wall, ball, slow, lawn, allow.

They teased Rudolph and covered him with white fluffy snow.

He couldn't play hide 'n' seek.

His shiny nose gave him away.

Santa Claus was going to choose his team.

It was a great honor to be chosen the sleigh guide.

Everyone was excited except Rudolph. He began to cry.

Working up, down, across, back and diagonally, circle the names of Santa's reindeer.
DASHER
BLITZEN
DANCER
VIXEN
CUPID
DONNER
COMET
PRANCER
B Z T N E Z T I L B
C R R O D O E P H P
X D L M I X R W X R
R A A N P K G L Y A
E S O N U G J V R N
N H C U C O M E T C
N E R X O E C L X E
O R C Z S N R Q T R
D B V I X E N A Z B

Santa wanted to be sure that the best reindeer was chosen.

Find the elf twins.
1
2
3
4
?
5
6
7
8
Answer: 4 and 7

PINE TREE MAZE

Color the star on top of each tree that adds up to 15.

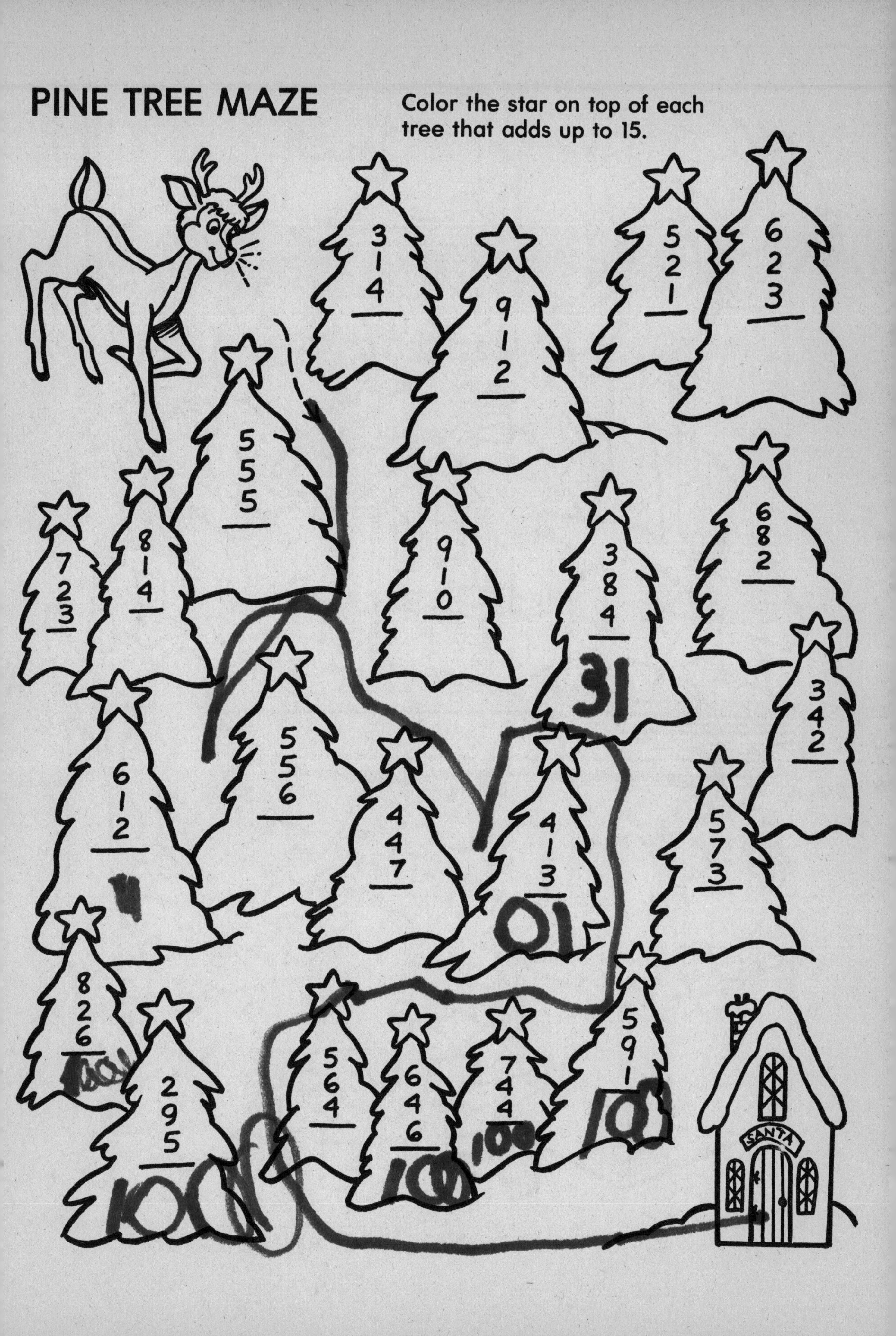

Everyone worked quickly.

Christmas would soon be here.

CHRISTMAS TOYS

ACROSS

2. These are made from wood.
4. This is used in the snow.
6. Billy's favorite toy
7. A stuffed toy.
8. These are fun to play.

DOWN

1. Betsy's favorite toy.
3. A musical instrument
4. Use on ice.
5. We use these for tea parties.
6. This toy spins.
7. We read these.

Answers: ACROSS: 2. blocks 4. sled 6. truck 7. bear 8. games
DOWN: 1. doll 3. drum 4. skates 5. dishes 6. top 7. books

Draw your favorite toy.

Santa packed his sack.

The elves were good helpers.

MAKING WRAPPING PAPER

You will need:

potato
knife
pencil with eraser
red or green stamp pad
or paper towel pads soaked
with red and green food
coloring.
newsprint or shelf paper.

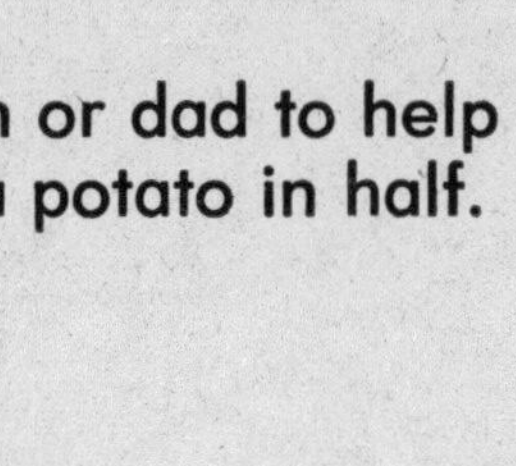

Ask mom or dad to help
you cut a potato in half.

Cut a tree shape on
one half of the potato.

Stamp potato on ink pad.
Press potato design on
paper as shown for pattern 1.

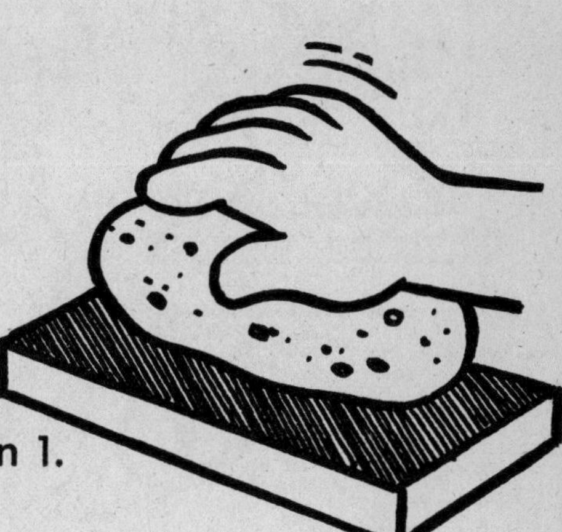

Dip pencil eraser in
red or green food coloring
for the design shown for
pattern 2.

Mrs. Claus baked Christmas treats.

CHRISTMAS TREATS

ACROSS

2. Santa wears a red one.
3. We make a lot of these for Christmas.
6. Elephants like these.
8. Candy bars are made from this.
10. We hang these on the Christmas tree.
11. Salty treats.

DOWN

1. Tiny cakes.
4. A chocolate candy.
5. A cool fruit drink.
7. This makes a popping sound while cooking.
9. This is used for sandwiches.

Answers: ACROSS: 2. suit 3. cookies 6. peanuts 8. chocolate 10. candy canes 11. pretzels DOWN: 1. cupcakes 4. fudge 5. punch 7. popcorn 9. bread

It was time to load the sleigh.

Rudolph wanted to help.

Dasher and Dancer were angry.

"Stop quarreling, you two!"

Color the spaces with one dot brown, to see who will appear.

Rudolph's nose provided light for Santa to read his list of good girls and boys.

Working up, down, across, back and diagonally, circle the names listed below.

"You will guide my sleigh tonight."

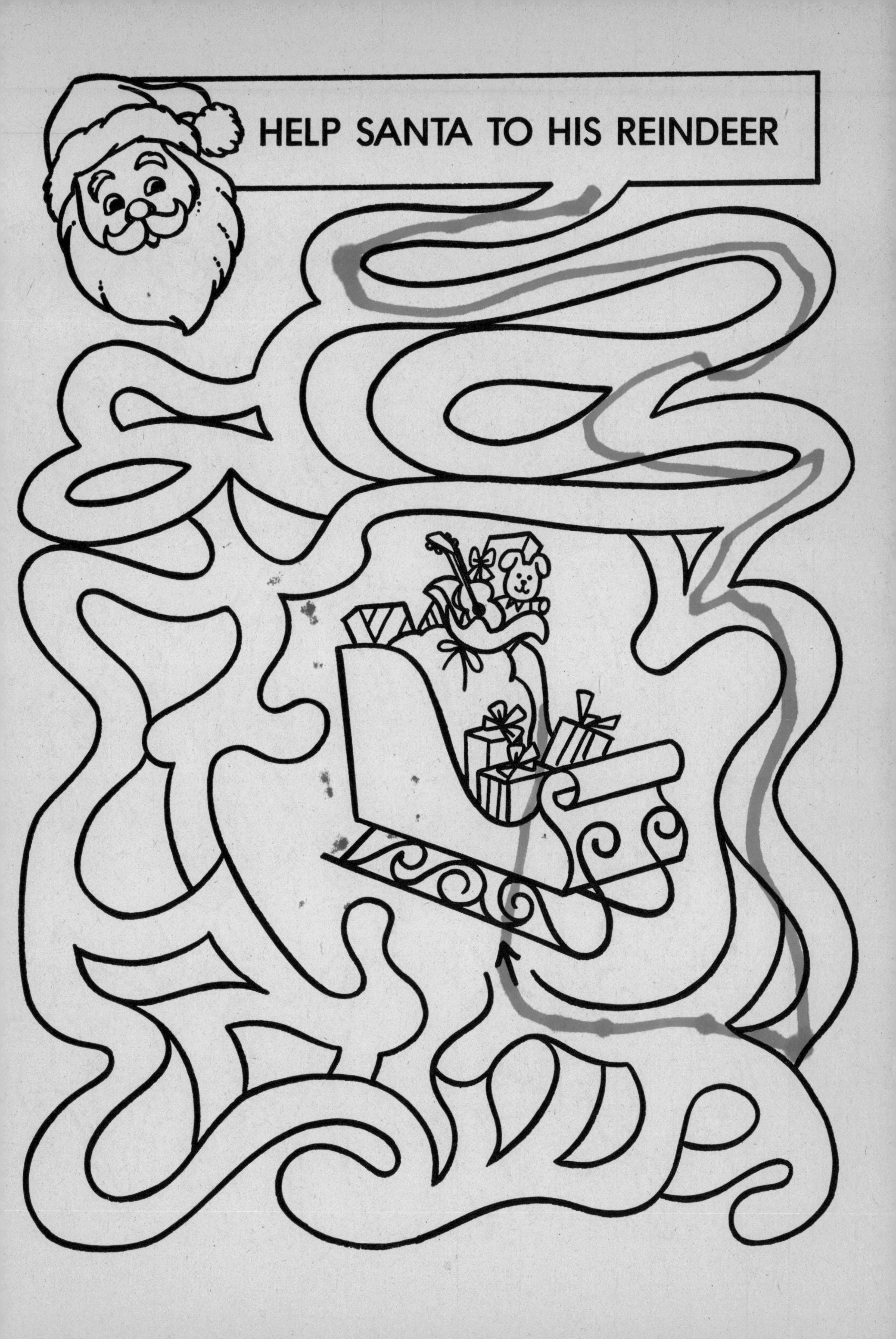
HELP SANTA TO HIS REINDEER

FIND THE MATCHING REINDEER

Draw lines to the matching reindeer.
One reindeer is left. Color his nose red.

NUMBER FUN

Santa has to go the same distance in every direction. Can you fill in the squares with numbers from one to nine so that each row, across, down or diagonally, add up to 15? Do not use any number twice.

2	9	4
7	5	3
6	1	8

"Have a safe trip!"

Christmas Eve Game

Color and cut out playing pieces and place on start. (One for each player.) Flip a coin; heads moves one space and tails moves two spaces. Follow directions on the individual spaces. The player to reach Santa's workshop first, is the winner. (You don't need the exact number to land on the last square.)

PLAYING PIECES

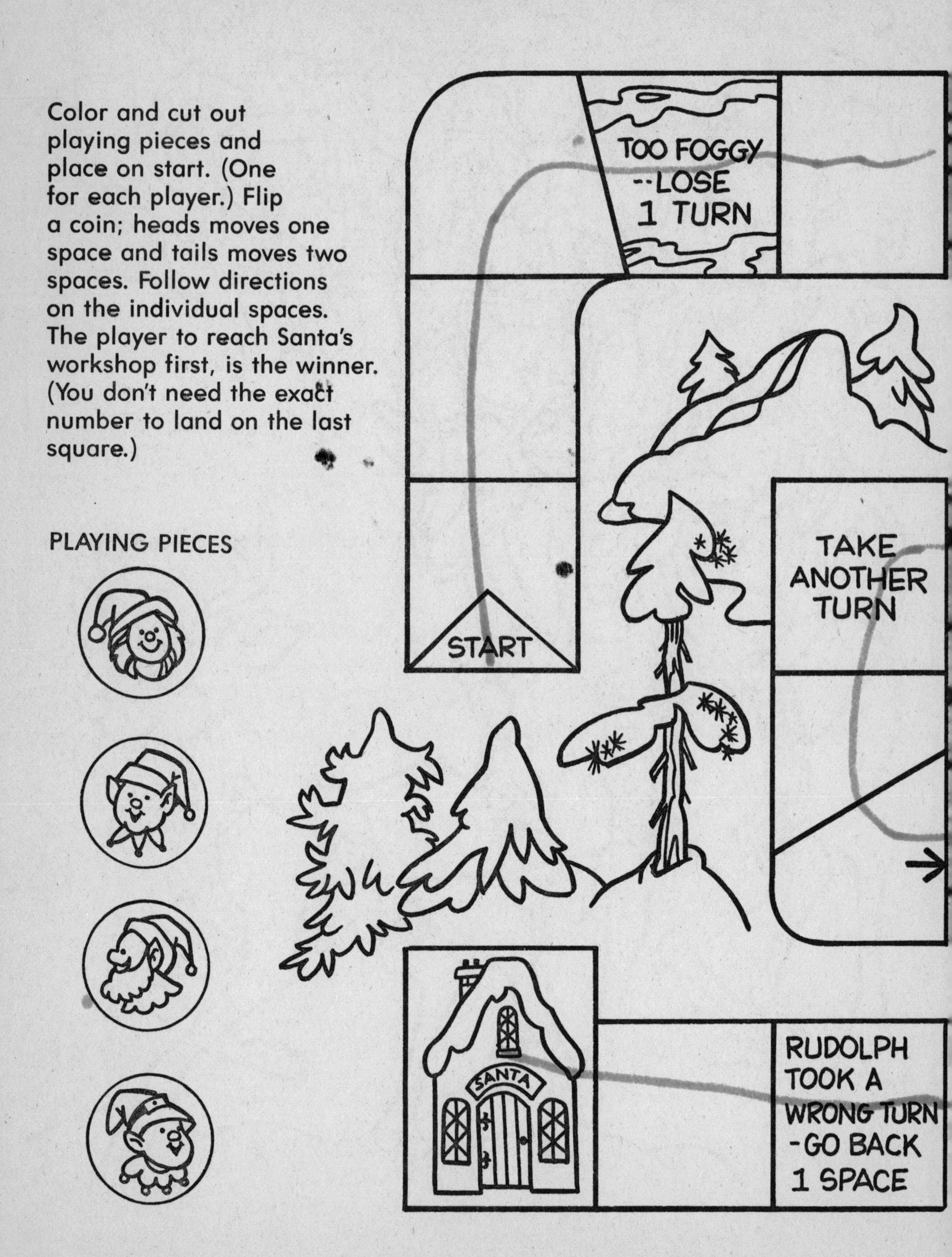

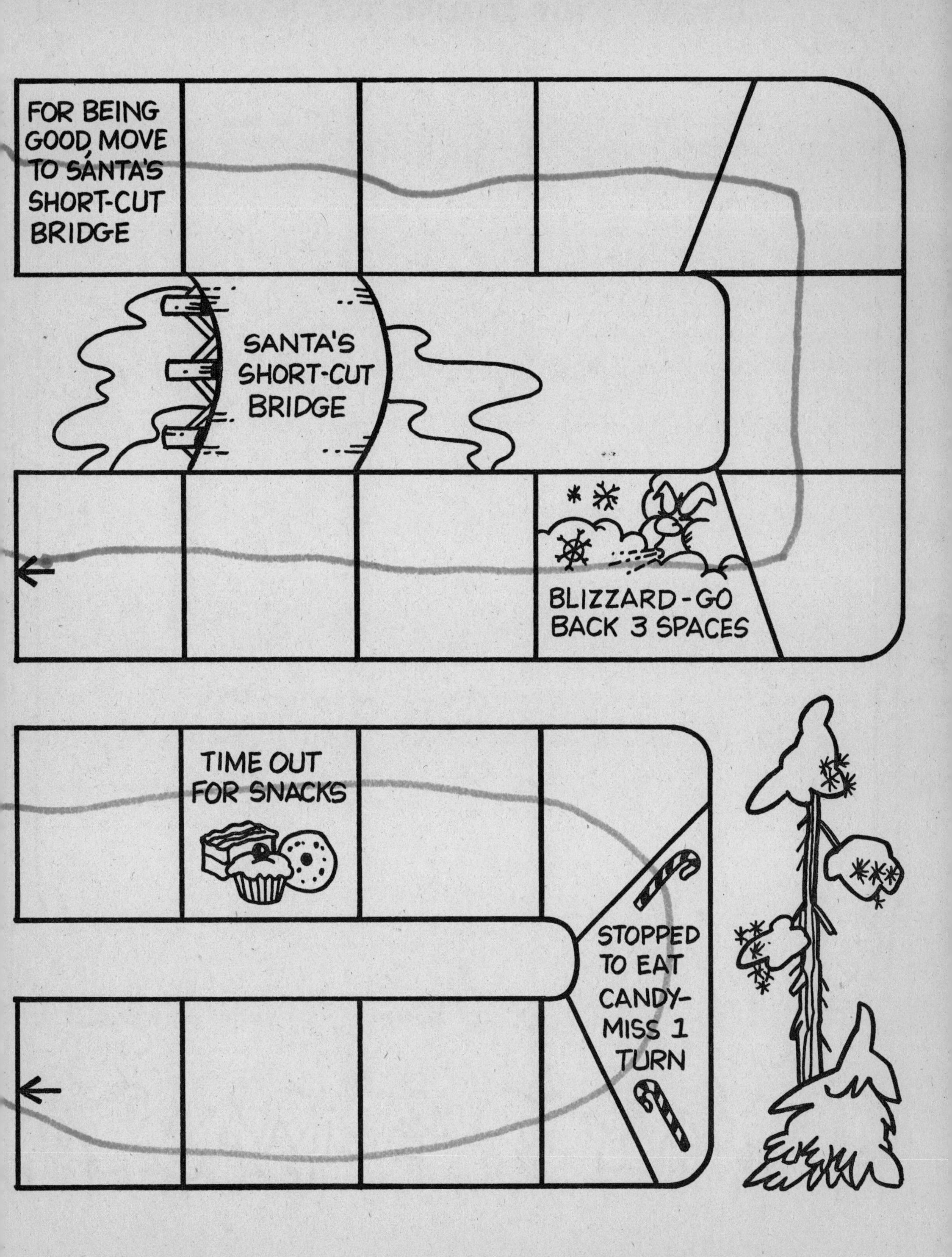
FOR BEING GOOD, MOVE TO SANTA'S SHORT-CUT BRIDGE
SANTA'S SHORT-CUT BRIDGE
BLIZZARD-GO BACK 3 SPACES
TIME OUT FOR SNACKS
STOPPED TO EAT CANDY-MISS 1 TURN

Draw your house for Santa.

Please help Santa find Billy's house. It's the one that is different from the rest.

Answer: 4

Santa left fruit and nuts for. . .

. . .the sleepy little forest animals.

"Welcome home, Santa!"

Rudolph was a hero.

What did Rudolph have for a treat?

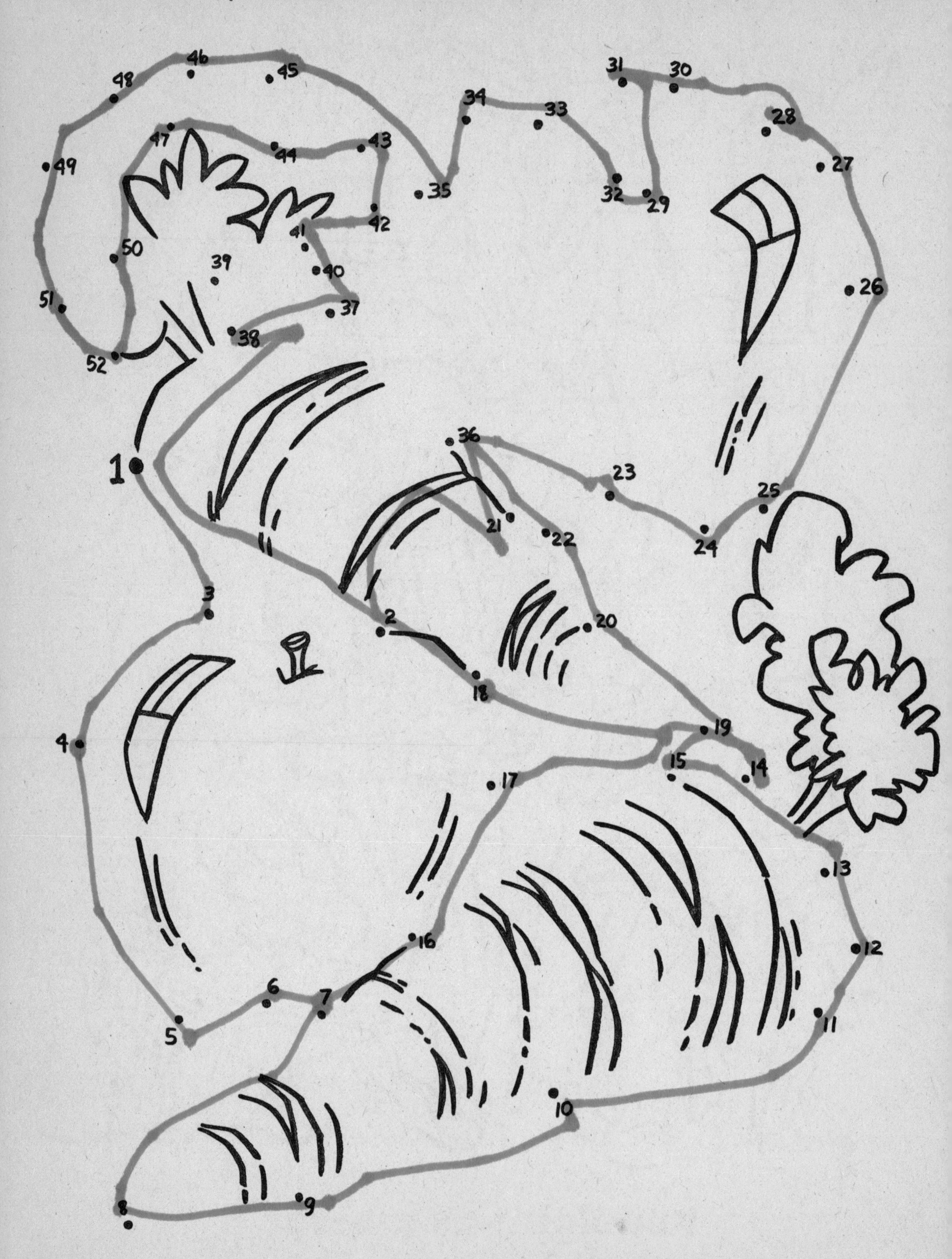

Santa had a treat for the reindeer. It's a treat you can eat, too.

REINDEER NIBBLES

1 box thin pretzels
1 box cereal of round oat cereal
1 box wheat or rice cereal.
I can salted peanuts.

Put all ingredients into roaster pan and toss to mix. Sprinkle with salt and garlic salt.

Take 1 stick of melted butter, 2 tablesoons of worcestershire sauce, 2 tablespoons of soy sauce and pour over mixture.
Toss again and bake at 325° for about one hour, stirring every 15 minutes.